FREDERICK DOUGLASS

YOUNG DEFENDER
OF HUMAN RIGHTS

Written by
Elisabeth P. Myers

Illustrated by Cathy Morrison

ISBN 978-1-882859-57-3 hardback
ISBN 978-1-882859-58-0 paperback

Patria Press, Inc.
PO Box 752
Carmel IN 46082
www.patriapress.com

Printed and bound in the United States of America
10 9 8 7 6 5 4 3 2 1

Text originally published by the Bobbs-Merrill Company, 1970, in the Childhood of Famous Americans Series®. The Childhood of Famous Americans Series® is a registered trademark of Simon & Schuster, Inc.

Library of Congress Cataloging-in-Publication Data

Myers, Elisabeth P.
  Frederick Douglass : young defender of human rights / by Elisabeth P. Myers ; illustrated by Cathy Morrison.–2nd ed.
    p. cm.–(Young patriots series v. 13)
  ISBN-13: 978-1-882859-57-3 (hardcover)
  ISBN-10: 1-882859-57-X (hardcover)
  ISBN-13: 978-1-882859-58-0 (pbk.)
  ISBN-10: 1-882859-58-8 (pbk.)
  1.   Douglass, Frederick, 1818-1895–Juvenile literature. 2. Abolitionists–United States--Biography–Juvenile literature. 3. African American abolitionists–Biography–Juvenile literature. 4. Antislavery movements–United States–Juvenile literature. I. Morrison, Cathy, ill. II. Title. III. Series.

  E449.D768M94 2007
  973.8092--dc22
  [B]   2006020702

Edited by Harold Underdown
Design by: Timothy Mayer/TM Design

This book is printed on Glatfelter's 55# Natural recycled paper.

Contents

		Page
1	Life with Aunt Betsey	1
2	New Faces and New Places	10
3	Asking for Trouble	21
4	Somebody's Child	31
5	Fred Learns a Hard Lesson	39
6	A Little Bit of Kindness	48
7	Fred Takes a Trip	55
8	A Child Like Any Other	64
9	A Giant Step	71
10	Fred Gets Ideas	77
11	A Stubborn Mule Needs Gentling	85
12	Fred Turns Teacher	92
13	North to Freedom and a New Life	99
	What Happened Next?	106
	Fun Facts about Frederick Douglass	107
	When Frederick Douglass Lived	108
	What Does That Mean?	111
	About the Author	113

Illustrations

Aunt Betsey came ashore, her net half full
of small, wriggly fish.   8

Many men and women were working in the fields,
their arms and bodies bending and twisting.   13

Sometimes one child's pebble would hit another's
pebble and knock it out of a square.   17

Fred was fascinated by the routine, as
Uncle Abel smoothed the leather. . .   29

His mother sat down in a rocker by the fire.   35

The raccoons also allowed Fred to hold
and stroke them. . .   41

. . .Colonel Lloyd raised his horsewhip and
slapped it down on Old Barney's bare shoulders.   45

Fred's heart gave a great leap.   51

Fred spent most of the day looking out
across the water.   61

Darkness was beginning to fall as the
sloop moved away from the dock.   63

"It's unsafe to teach a slave to read."   70

Both people and animals, Fred learned, had to
be closely examined to determine their value.   75

So this was writing!   83

. . .except that he was "stubborn as a mule
and needed gentling."   89

"We are betrayed!"   97

At first his voice cracked as he spoke. . .   104

For my grandson, Phillip

Chapter 1

Life with Aunt Betsey

Five-year-old Fred Bailey knelt on the hard-packed dirt outside the cabin. He held a kernel of corn between his brown fingers. "Come squirrel, squirrel!" he said softly, making a soft chirruping sound in his throat.

A red squirrel, running along the rail fence, stopped and flicked its tail. Fred chirruped again, and the squirrel jumped to the ground. Then Fred held himself still, and the squirrel inched itself closer to him step by careful step.

A slight noise from the cabin broke the spell. The squirrel scampered away even before Fred's grandmother, Aunt Betsey Bailey, appeared in the doorway with a large wooden bucket.

"Here, Fred," she said. "Will you take this bucket and get me some water from the well?"

Fred popped the kernel of corn into his mouth and ran to his grandmother. "Yes, I'll get some water," he said proudly, taking the bucket from his grandmother's outstretched hands.

He went to the well and lowered the bucket in, then brought it up brimming full of water. He unhooked the bucket carefully, trying not to spill any of the water. As he trudged slowly toward the cabin, a little water sloshed over his dusty hands.

"That's fine, Fred," his grandmother called encouragingly.

She spoke a moment too soon. Suddenly Fred stumbled over a tree root in his path. He kept a tight hold on the bucket, but most of the water spilled on the ground.

Aunt Betsey made a clicking sound with her tongue. "You're lucky Old Master wasn't around to see you, Fred," she said, "or you'd get a licking for sure."

Fred shivered. He had never seen the person Aunt Betsey referred to, but he knew he and his grandmother both belonged to a man named Captain Anthony. They were the man's slaves, and he could do whatever he wanted to do with them. He could even take Fred away from his grandmother.

"When you're big enough, you'll have to go to the home place," Aunt Betsey told all the children in her care.

This home place was a large Maryland plantation situated on the River Wye. It was the largest of many farms owned by Colonel Edward Lloyd. Fred's master,

Captain Anthony, was chief clerk for Colonel Lloyd, though he owned several farms in Talbot County himself.

Aunt Betsey had worked hard for Captain Anthony for many years. When she grew too old to do field work, he had moved her to a cabin on one of his most distant farms. There she cared for all the babies born to his slave women. More often than not, these babies were her grandchildren, but he didn't realize this. If he had known, he would have made other plans for them. He separated children from their mothers to break their family ties.

Fred, having been placed in his grandmother's care, was luckier than many other enslaved children. Aunt Betsey cared for him lovingly, and he loved her in return. He respected and admired her, too, because she was held in high esteem in the neighborhood. Also, she had a reputation for being a very skilled fisherwoman. The shad and herring just seemed to jump into her nets.

Aunt Betsey was the only mother Fred had known. He didn't remember ever seeing his mother. She came occasionally to visit Aunt Betsey, but always after Fred was fast asleep. This was the only time she could come because she was hired out as a field hand to a Mr. Stewart, who lived many miles away. Unless she could somehow borrow a mule to ride, she couldn't cover the distance back and forth in time to be present for roll call at dawn.

Fred turned back toward the well with the bucket. This time he transferred the full bucket safely to his grandmother's hands. He followed her into the cabin and watched as she poured the water into a large black pot. She hung the pot from an iron hook dangling from a crane and swung it into the fireplace, where a small fire was burning.

"While the water's coming to a boil, we'll go down to the river to catch us a mess of herring," Aunt Betsey said.

"Both of us?" cried Fred. His grandmother seldom invited him to go fishing.

"You're the only person I see around," Aunt Betsey answered.

Fred clapped his hands. "I'll go get the new net!" he cried.

He could see the net she had finished making the night before, hanging from a post of her pine bedstead. It looked to him just like the oriole's nest that swung in a willow tree near the river.

"I was thinking of selling this new net," his grandmother objected.

Selling nets which she made was almost the only way she had of making money. She had a reputation for making nets strong and tight and could sell them in the villages thereabouts.

"Do you have to sell the net?" asked Fred. He hoped that Aunt Betsey didn't need the money from the sale of one net now and could wait until allowance day.

At the end of each month, the enslaved people from the different farms got their monthly allowance of salt, corn, and pickled pork at the "home place." The amount given was never generous, and especially not to a slave like Aunt Betsey, who did not work in the fields. The allotment for the children in her care was even less.

So Aunt Betsey not only fished but raised a little patch of sweet potatoes, and she always had food for hungry stomachs. The few pennies she made from selling her fishnets went for molasses or some other kind of sweetening. She always bought the molasses at the end of the month, when she had an excuse to pass through the village.

"I'll see," Aunt Betsey said in answer to Fred's question.

She couldn't read, but she could count and she kept a calendar of sorts. Her calendar was a square of clay beside the fireplace, where she scratched a little line every day with a sharp stick. At the beginning of each month she rubbed out the lines and started fresh on the new month.

The fire was not very bright, but except for the open door, it provided the only light in the windowless log cabin. Aunt Betsey had to kneel with her face very close to the hearth in order to see her scratches. When she looked at them she found that the month was only half over. This meant she would have time to make other nets to sell.

"You can get the new net," she told Fred.

Standing on tiptoe, Fred lifted the net carefully from the bedpost. He hugged it tightly against his body, afraid he might catch it on something and tear it.

"I declare, a person would think you are carrying a baby," his grandmother said.

They walked down the hill on which the cabin stood. In the valley below, beside the river, they came to a water mill, where the villagers brought their corn to be ground into meal. One of Fred's favorite pastimes was watching the huge millwheel turn slowly round and round. Watching the wheel was also a favorite pastime of the other children in Aunt Betsey's household. Two of them were watching it now as Fred and his grandmother came by. Two others were trying to fish in the millpond with string and hooks made of bent wire.

"Where are you going?" the children cried with one voice.

"We're going fishing," said Fred, who knew from

experience that they wouldn't catch anything with their baitless hooks.

"May we go, too?" asked the others, but Aunt Betsey shook her head.

"So many of you together would scare the fish away," she said. "You may go sometime later. Just wait awhile."

Fred took his grandmother's hand and squeezed it. She squeezed back, then freed herself. "Come," she said. "We're wasting time."

She walked on downstream, until suddenly she changed her course and waded into the water up to her waist. Fred started to follow her, but the current pulled at his legs and he felt frightened. "It's too strong for me," he said. He started to cry because he had wanted to hold one end of the new net.

"There's nothing to cry about," Aunt Betsey said, coming to take the net. "The rains have flooded the river, that's all. I'm having a little trouble myself."

Fred went back to the bank and sat down. After a few minutes, he started to pick the daisies that grew within arm's reach. When he had a lap full of them, he plaited their stems together to make a crown.

He was still working on the crown when Aunt Betsey came ashore, her net half full of small, wriggly fish. "We have enough for supper and some to salt down," she said.

Aunt Betsey came ashore, her net half full of small, wriggly fish. "We have enough for supper and some to salt down."

Fred got up, careless of the daisies that scattered around him. He looked gloatingly at his grandmother's catch. "That's surely a fine mess of fish," he said, licking his lips as if already tasting the fish stew he would have for supper. He was hungry, even though he'd had a cold sweet potato to eat at midday.

The thought of the stew lent wings to Fred's feet. He raced on ahead of his grandmother but stopped short at the top of the hill. In front of the cabin he saw a horse-drawn wagon with a white man sitting on the seat.

Fred rushed back to tell his grandmother. "We have company, Grandmother," he cried. "There's a white man waiting in a wagon. What do you suppose he wants?"

Aunt Betsey put her free hand up to her eyes as if to shade them. "I don't have to suppose, Fred," she said, and her voice sounded as if it were cracking. "I'm afraid I know."

She quickened her steps. Fred ran to keep up with her and tugged at her skirt. "What's the matter, Grandmother?" he asked anxiously. "What is it?"

Aunt Betsey freed herself gently. "You'll find out soon enough," she said. "Now run away and play until I call you." As Fred stopped in the path, confused, she walked on toward the cabin and the man waiting for her in the wagon.

Chapter 2

New Faces
and New Places

Fred hurried back down to the water mill to tell the other children about their grandmother's visitor. They all wanted to see the stranger for themselves, but they knew Aunt Betsey would be angry if they came near.

They watched from the hill, and for a while there was nothing to see but the horse and wagon. The man had gone into the cabin to talk with Aunt Betsey. "I hope she doesn't forget about our fish stew," Fred said.

"I hope the stranger isn't eating it," said one of his cousins.

This dreadful thought made all the children gasp. Just then the man appeared and drove quickly away, without sparing a nod for Aunt Betsey, who stood in the doorway.

Aunt Betsey stared at the cloud of dust he left in his wake, not moving until the sound of the wheels died away. Then, making a megaphone with her hands around her mouth, she called, "Children! You may come now!"

The fish stew was good and hot, and she gave them bits of corn bread to eat with it. She never mentioned the visitor, and somehow Fred and his cousins knew that she didn't intend to, at least not then.

Days passed, and the memory of the visitor dimmed. Fred would have forgotten him entirely, except that since his visit, Grandmother seemed different. Somehow she was quieter. She didn't sing quite so often. Occasionally, when Fred was lying in the loft, half awake, half asleep, he heard her make moaning sounds. Could she be sick, he wondered?

One summer morning, a few weeks later, Aunt Betsey roused all the children early. "Fred and I are going for a long walk," she said. "Mr. Lee, at the mill, is going to keep an eye on the rest of you. Do what he tells you to do."

She gave Fred the linen shirt which she had washed and ironed for him after he had gone to bed the night before. She wound a crisp white bandanna turban around her head. She packed some food for them. Then she sent all the children outside, stepped out herself, and closed the cabin door firmly behind her.

Fred felt all tingly. He and Grandmother must be going a long way, because she almost never closed that door in the summer time.

Aunt Betsey didn't explain. She just set out down the road, without even looking back to see whether he was following her. He had to run to stay near her. Soon his legs became tired and he began to lag farther and farther behind. Finally she turned back and picked him up. Being carried made him feel ashamed, and he said, "I'm not a baby, Grandmother! Put me down, please!"

Grandmother put him back down. "Try to keep up then," she said. "We're still a long way from where we're going."

The road grew less and less open and finally ran into a forest. Fred was glad to be where it was dark and cool. The glare of the sun on the unshaded road had made him very hot.

In a clearing, where there was a brook, Aunt Betsey stopped. "We'll have something to eat and sit for a while," she said. "Put your feet in the water to rest them."

Fred was barefoot, as usual, because he had no shoes. He also had no stockings, jacket, or pants, nor was he likely to have any for years. The only clothing an enslaved child had until he was old enough to work in the field was a long shirt, which hung to his knees. Two shirts a year each was the allowance for both boys and girls, winter and summer.

Many men and women were working in the fields, their arms and bodies bending and twisting. They seemed to be keeping time to the songs they were singing.

Aunt Betsey's sitting spell lasted only a few minutes. Then she was up and trudging on, and Fred had no choice but to follow.

They left the woods behind and came to huge fields of wheat, rye, oats, corn, and tobacco which stretched out in every direction. Many men and women were working in the fields, their arms and bodies bending and twisting. They seemed to be keeping time to the songs they were singing.

Fred was interested in what he saw, because everything was different from the country around Aunt Betsey's cabin. The soil in her neighborhood was too poor for farming. The people there had little means of making a living except by fishing in the river.

"Those workers seem to be having fun," Fred said to his grandmother.

Aunt Betsey snorted. "Don't be fooled by their singing, child," she said. "They have to sing while they work. Overseers are afraid that quiet slaves might be thinking, and thinking could lead to trouble."

"How, Grandmother?" Fred asked, but Aunt Betsey didn't answer.

The shadows grew longer and longer as the afternoon advanced. At last Aunt Betsey walked between two big stone posts into a deeply rutted cart road, and Fred guessed they had almost reached their destination. He was glad, because he was very, very tired.

The cart road ended in a great yard filled with both noisy children and noisy animals. The children varied in color from black, brown, and copper-colored to almost white. The animals included chickens, ducks, and other feathered creatures, dogs and cats, and even a little curly-tailed pig. They made such a racket with their clucking and quacking, their bow-wowing and their squealing, that Fred held his hands over his ears.

Aunt Betsey took one of his hands and led him up a few steps into a big room. There a black woman was cutting vegetables into a bowl. She stopped when she saw them coming.

"Is this the new boy, Betsey?" she said, nodding at Fred, who moved closer to Aunt Betsey.

Aunt Betsey nodded in answer. "Yes, and his name is Fred."

"Fred," the other woman said. "Well, you may call me Aunt Katy."

Fred did not answer. He only stood and looked at the floor.

"Is he stubborn?" asked Aunt Katy.

"No, he's a good boy," Aunt Betsey said. She smoothed Fred's stubbly head. "Go out now and play with the other children."

"I'd rather stay here," Fred said.

Aunt Betsey took him to the door. Then she pointed to some of the children and said, "Those are your brothers and sisters. The others are cousins like the children back in Tuckahoe. Go and play with them."

She gave him a little push and he walked reluctantly down the steps. At first, the children were so busy playing some kind of game with pebbles that they didn't notice him. They were having so much fun he was curious and moved closer to see what they were playing.

The children had drawn a number of squares in the hard-packed dirt and were tossing pebbles into them. Sometimes one child's pebble would hit another's pebble and knock it out of a square. Then there were shouts of glee and cries of disappointment.

One of the children whom Aunt Betsey had pointed out as Fred's sister finally noticed him and smiled. "You're Fred and I'm Sarah," she said. "We have the same mammy."

The other children stopped playing. They crowded around Fred, giving him their names as Sarah had done. His brother's name was Perry and another sister's name was Eliza.

"Do you want to play?" Perry asked. "Here, take my shooters. I'll get some more."

Fred was surprised but took the three pebbles that Perry handed him. They were warm from Perry's fingers, and smooth.

Perry immediately darted off to the stone driveway that led to the front of the house. He returned shortly, clutching a new supply of pebbles. "I didn't get caught," he said with evident pride to the other children.

Fred was puzzled by this remark. "Get caught by what?" he asked.

"By anybody," Perry answered, but made no further explanation.

Fred was used to grown-ups giving no answer or only a partial answer. But Perry wasn't a grown-up.

Sometimes one child's pebble
would hit another's pebble
and knock it out of a square.

17

"Who is anybody?" he persisted.

The children looked at one another and Sarah shook her head slightly. "Oh, just one of the uncles," Perry finally said.

The answer didn't help Fred very much. In slave talk, "Uncle" and "Aunt" didn't mean kinship. They were titles of respect.

"Let's play," said Sarah quickly. "Fred can go first." She showed Fred how to step up to the line to get ready to shoot. "Keep track of all the stones you have," she warned. "The player who has the most stones left after everybody has shot is the winner."

Fred nodded. He had already guessed that having the most stones was important. "Toe up," said the other children, crowding around.

Fred toed up to the line and tossed. His first two pebbles bounced into a square and out. "You throw too hard," Eliza said.

Thanks to her warning, Fred's last shot was successful. The stone stayed smack in the middle of the center square. He could not hold back letting out an exclamation of pleasure. "Next time I throw the pebbles I'll get all of them in!" he promised himself.

The very next child to shoot knocked Fred's pebble out of the square and he didn't have a chance to throw again. By now the other children were tired of playing and suggested looking for windfalls.

Fred knew that the children meant apples, peaches, and pears that had fallen from the trees. Usually windfalls rotted easily. A person was lucky if he got a few good bites from one, but they were the only fruit that Fred had ever tasted.

His mouth watered at the idea of biting into a juicy peach or pear, however damaged it might be. Many hours had passed since he and his grandmother had eaten fish and bread in the forest. Even so, he didn't want to go off anyplace where his grandmother couldn't find him when she was ready to leave.

Sarah came and took him by the hand. "Come on. It isn't far," she said, and pulled him so that he had to go along.

They hadn't been at the orchard long, when a child came running from the house. "Fred! Fred!" he cried. "Your grandmother is gone!"

"No!" Fred cried. With tears streaming down his cheeks, he hurried to see for himself. When he reached the kitchen yard, he ran up the steps into the house.

Inside the kitchen he found Aunt Katy all alone, cutting up vegetables as before. He didn't wait to ask where his grandmother was but turned and ran out again. This time he ran a little way down the cart path along which he and she had come to the house.

Aunt Betsey was nowhere in sight. Fred lay down in the path and sobbed and sobbed. Soon Sarah and

Perry and Eliza came and knelt down beside him. "Don't cry," they said, and offered him peaches and pears.

Fred wouldn't be comforted. "She didn't even say good-bye!" he wailed.

"She couldn't," Sarah said. "Old Master wouldn't have wanted her to."

"Old Master!" Fred repeated. He sat up with a jerk. "Is this the home place?"

Sarah stared at him. "Why, of course it is. You mean that you didn't know?"

Fred shook his head.

"Well, now you know," Perry said. "If you're smart, you'll stop crying. Otherwise you might get a licking the very first day you are here."

All Fred could do was shake his head again.

Chapter 3

Asking for Trouble

The clanging of a bell brought frightened looks to the faces of Fred's brother and sisters. "Aunt Katy is waiting for us," Perry said. "If we don't hurry, we won't get any supper!"

Fred felt too sick to want anything to eat, but he knew he couldn't stay where he was. He took the outstretched hands of his two sisters and walked between them to the house, crying as he went.

Aunt Katy was waiting on the kitchen stoop. She glared at Fred and said, "It won't do any good for you to cry for your grandmother. You will probably never see her again."

Fred broke out in a fresh burst of crying. Aunt Katy reached out a skinny arm and yanked him into the house. "I won't stand for all this foolish crying," she said.

With these words she shoved Fred into a closet that opened off the kitchen. He fell to his knees on a rough dirt floor. "For that, you'll go hungry tonight," she said. Then she closed the door, leaving him in darkness.

Fred lay where he had fallen. He could not help continuing to cry, but he stifled the sound against his bare arm. Gradually, his eyes grew heavy and he fell asleep.

The next morning Aunt Katy opened the door to rouse him and he sprang to his feet. "Are you ready to be sensible?" she asked.

Fred nodded, and she looked at him. "Does the cat have your tongue?" she asked.

"No, ma'am," said Fred, shaking his head.

"That's better," she said. "Now you can eat, and this once I'll give you a head start on all the other children."

She pointed to a sort of trough, filled with a mixture of coarse cornmeal and water. Fred hesitated, because he saw nothing to eat with.

"What's the matter?" Aunt Katy asked sharply. "Are you too proud to eat your meals with your hands?"

Again Fred shook his head. "No, ma'am," he said. He cupped both hands together, scooped up some mush, and poured it into his mouth. Then he chewed, swallowed, and scooped up some more. He repeated the same routine until trampling footsteps outside warned of the other children's approach.

"That's enough," Aunt Katy said when she heard the sound. "Step aside now."

Fred was still hungry, but he did as Aunt Katy had said. He wiped his mouth on his sleeve and his hands on his shirttail. Immediately the other children rushed to find places at the feeding trough. Within a few minutes the trough was empty.

"Now go back outdoors," said Aunt Katy.

The other children left, but Fred lingered inside. He didn't know what was expected of him. Would Aunt Katy tell him? Or would Captain Anthony, the old master whom he had heard so much about, come to tell him?

"Didn't you hear me tell you to get out?" Aunt Katy said, brandishing a cooking spoon.

This time Fred didn't bother to answer. He scooted for the open door, where Sarah and Perry were waiting for him. "We'll show you around," they said. "Then if you get sent somewhere, you'll know where to go."

Fred was eager to see what this strange place was like. So far, all he had seen of the home place were a kitchen and a yard. He supposed they were part of Captain Anthony's house, and he was nearly right. As long as Captain Anthony remained Colonel Lloyd's chief clerk, he would live in the substantial brick house containing Aunt Katy's kitchen.

Captain Anthony's house stood on a little hill in the center of the plantation village. Below his house were a great many other habitations. One of these, called the "Long Quarter," was a long, low, rough building, housing slaves of all ages, conditions, and sizes. Another tall and rickety building served as a dormitory for hundreds of other slaves. There were also dozens of little log and mud huts, similar to the cabin where Fred had lived at Tuckahoe.

"Who lives down there?" Fred asked.

"House servants, mostly," said Sarah, "or any other slaves Mr. Sevier favors."

"Who is Mr. Sevier?" Fred asked next.

"The overseer," Perry answered. "He's the man in charge of Colonel Lloyd's slaves."

Perry's words puzzled Fred. "What do you mean by Colonel Lloyd's slaves?" he asked. "Aren't we his slaves too?"

"Of course not," said Perry. "We belong to Old Master."

Still Fred didn't understand, so this time Sarah chimed in. "None of Old Master's working slaves live here," she explained. "They're on his farms, in Tuckahoe, or rented out someplace. We children aren't big enough to work, so he puts us in Aunt Katy's charge."

This worried Fred. He had a feeling that he had

started off on the wrong foot with Aunt Katy. "Who is in charge of Aunt Katy?" he asked.

"Just Old Master," Sarah explained. "She's to him what he is to Colonel Lloyd. So with all of us children, her word is law."

They had passed the slave houses now and were in the business part of the village. All around were storehouses, tobacco houses, and barns. There also were blacksmith's shops, wheelwright's shops, and cooper's shops—more kinds of shops than Fred had ever seen before.

The roaring of the forge fire, the whirr of turning wheels, the banging of hammers interested Fred. He would have liked to stay and watch each man work, but Sarah and Perry kept urging him on. "You haven't seen the Great House yet," they cried.

When they reached it, Fred gasped at the sight of the immense three-storied white frame house with wings on three sides. In front, there was a large two-storied portico or veranda, supported by a long line of white columns that extended the entire length of the building.

"There's where we get the pebbles for our game," said Perry, pointing to the driveway leading up to the house.

Fred looked at the wide drive. It formed a circle around a beautiful green lawn and led off between overhanging shade trees toward a distant ornamental gate. The lawn was planted with blossoming shrubs and flowers, all lending sweet perfume to the air.

For a moment, Fred stared at the beautiful scene. Then he was not able to stand just looking any longer. He darted across the drive and stooped to stroke the smooth green grass. Then suddenly he saw an older white boy standing directly in front of him. "Why are you here?" asked the boy. "What were you doing?"

"I was just feeling the grass," Fred said. "I never saw such pretty grass before."

"You ought to lie down on it," the other boy said as he lay down to demonstrate. "Come on and try it!" he invited.

Fred hesitated, but his curiosity was so great that he lay down, too. The beautiful grass made the softest bed he had ever known, and it smelled fresh and sweet. As he lay there, he was happier than he had been any time since his grandmother had left.

"I'm Daniel Lloyd," the white boy said.

At once Fred was filled with fright. He was lying on the grass with the son of the plantation owner! He had been invited, but he knew he shouldn't be there.

Quickly he jumped up and looked over to where he had left Sarah and Perry. They were almost hidden behind tree trunks at the edge of the yard, as if trying to stay out of sight. "I have to go, Master Daniel," said

Fred, hurrying to rejoin his brother and sister.

The two children grasped his hands and pulled him hastily back toward the slave village. "You're just asking for trouble acting like that," Sarah scolded. "We're not allowed to play around the Big House!"

"Master Daniel invited me to lie on the grass," Fred said.

"He'll likely be sorry, too, if anybody saw you," Perry said.

They now were in the main village. Fred's attention was distracted by a rhythmic *tap! tap! tap!* nearby. He looked around, expecting to see a woodpecker drumming on a hollow log. "Uncle Abel's making shoes," Perry explained. "Let's go watch him for a minute."

They went into a small shed, where a round-shouldered little man sat astride a saddle-shaped bench. He was hammering nails into a piece of leather propped up on a foot-sized stand before him. When he saw the children, he paused.

"This is Fred Bailey, Uncle Abel," Sarah said.

Uncle Abel mumbled something through his mouthful of tacks. Then, realizing that he couldn't speak clearly, he spit the tacks into his hand.

"Are you another of Harriet's children?" he asked loudly and clearly.

"I guess so," replied Fred, for he knew his mother's name was Harriet.

"May we watch?" Perry asked.

Uncle Abel nodded. "I'm getting some shoes ready for next allowance day," he said.

He kept a few tacks loose in his hand. Then, popping the others back into his mouth, he returned to his job.

Fred was fascinated by the routine, as Uncle Abel smoothed the leather, inserted a tack, and hammered. His actions were as rhythmic as music, Fred thought. Smooth, insert, and hammer. Smooth, insert, and hammer!

Fred would have liked to watch the shoemaker for a long time, but the other children grew restless. "I'm hungry," Perry said. "Maybe Aunt Katy will give us some bread if we go to the kitchen and ask her politely."

The mere thought of bread made Fred's mouth water. He hadn't had anything to eat except a few scoops of mush since he had eaten lunch with his grandmother the noon before. He was hungry, but he wasn't hopeful about getting any bread.

Aunt Katy was beating a carpet spread out on the grass. When she saw Fred, she raised the broom and hit at him. "This is your first day here and already you're acting uppity!" she yelled.

Fred ducked and put his arms over his face to protect himself. He didn't ask what he had done to

Fred was fascinated by the routine, as Uncle Abel smoothed
the leather, inserted a tack, and hammered.

deserve this kind of treatment. He guessed that somehow word of his daring to lie on the grass had reached Aunt Katy.

"Get out of my sight and stay out!" Aunt Katy ordered. "And don't come around expecting any supper. I'll starve you into knowing your place around here, that's what I'll do!"

The only place where Fred knew to go to keep out of her sight was the little closet where she had shoved him the night before. He crept back in, lay down on the floor, and gave way to tears.

This time, he cried more from fright than from loneliness. Since he had no way of knowing what his place was, he was almost certain that Aunt Katy would starve him to death.

Chapter 4

Somebody's Child

Fred lay in the dark closet for a long time. Through cracks in the wall, he could peer out into the kitchen. What he saw and what he smelled almost tortured him. A whole skinned animal of some sort was turning on a spit over the fireplace. Great pots of something savory were steaming on the iron stove. At a table, Aunt Katy was mixing flour and water into a batter and rolling it flat. Then she filled the batter with sliced fruit and put it into a pan.

Fred had never seen or smelled such mouth-watering goodies before, but he knew better than to expect to get to eat any of them. They had to be for Old Master's table, and not for the slaves.

At sundown Aunt Katy rang the bell to call the other children to supper. A few minutes later she called Fred from his hiding place. His hopes rose. Maybe she hadn't meant what she said! Maybe she would give him something to eat after all.

She gave great chunks of corn bread and pieces of pork fat to the others, but gave nothing to Fred. His sisters gave him sad looks, but there was nothing they could do to help him. Aunt Katy kept them under her watchful eye until their food was gone.

After supper, most of the children went off to their sleeping places. Fred went outdoors, thinking perhaps he could go to the orchard and find some fruit to eat.

But it was night and there was no light to guide him. He groped his way back to the kitchen steps and sat down. Tears rolled down his cheeks again, and he was so miserable he wished that he could just fall asleep and wake up back at Aunt Betsey's.

For a time he could hear Aunt Katy moving in the kitchen, but after while everything became quiet. Cautiously he got up, peeked inside, and saw nobody.

Hope rose again. He looked all around the kitchen for some food, but all he could find was an ear of dried Indian corn on a shelf. He stood on tiptoe and managed to reach the ear. He tore off some kernels with his fingernails and put the cob good side forward on the shelf again. Then he shoved the loose corn into the still-warm ashes of the fire to roast.

By now Fred was so hungry that he snatched out some of the kernels before they were even warm. Before he could start eating, Aunt Katy came back into the kitchen with another woman. The woman looked at Fred and gave a little cry. "My little boy!" she said, hastening to throw her arms around him.

Fred did not know who the woman was, but her kind welcome started him crying again. The woman misinterpreted his tears. "Don't be afraid of me!" she said. "I'm your mother!"

"I'm not afraid of you," he said, sobbing. "I was afraid I would starve to death!" He raised a handful of kernels to his mouth.

His mother quickly dashed the kernels to the floor. "Nobody is going to threaten to starve my son!" she said, darting such a threatening look toward Aunt Katy that the cook almost seemed to shrink. "Get him something good to eat at once!"

Aunt Katy was stunned and unable to move. She just stood still, her mouth opening and closing like that of a new-caught fish.

"All right, I'll get him something myself!" Fred's mother said. She went to the larder and took down a beautiful, spicy-smelling cake and gave it to Fred.

Hungry though he was, Fred stared at the delicacy in his hand. It was heart shaped and covered on top with a dark sugary glaze. It was so pretty Fred could scarcely believe it was meant to be eaten.

His mother saw his hesitation. "Eat your gingerbread!" she said. "And when you finish, if you're still hungry, you can have some more."

At that Aunt Katy made a sharp, protesting sound, a kind of yip. Fred, afraid that she might snatch the gingerbread away, began hastily to eat. His mother sat down in a rocker by the fire. She pulled Fred onto her lap and cradled him fondly. Then, while he continued to eat, she gave Aunt Katy a tongue-lashing.

"If you ever threaten to starve my child to death again, I'll know about it," she said. "I'll learn about it the same way I learned he had been brought here. Also the next time I'll tell Old Master how you are treating him and you know what that will mean!"

Fred learned later that his mother was thought to be clairvoyant, a person who knew about things that were to happen before they took place. Right now, though, he could see that Aunt Katy was frightened by his mother's words. He guessed she would treat him less harshly, at least for a while.

That thought, plus the fullness of his stomach and the warmth of his mother's embrace, made Fred relax. His mother spoke to him softly from time to time and crooned to him. She sang the same lullaby his grandmother had sung to the newest baby in her cabin family.

"Hushabye,
Don't you cry,
Go to sleep, little baby;
When you wake
You shall have

His mother sat down in a rocker by the fire. She pulled
Fred onto her lap and cradled him fondly.

All the pretty little horses;
Blacks and bays,
Dapples and grays,
Coach and six little horses.
Hushabye,
Don't you cry,
Go to sleep, little baby."

Before his mother reached the refrain of the second verse, Fred was sound asleep. The next morning when he awoke, he was lying on the fireplace hearth. He rubbed his eyes, sat up, and looked about the room. Aunt Katy was the only person he saw. For a moment, he wondered if he had dreamed his mother had been there.

"It won't do you any good to look for your mother," Aunt Katy said. "She's gone."

Fred felt happier. Now he knew that seeing his mother the night before had not been a dream. He no longer was just a child, he was somebody's child. Even if he never saw his mother again, he would know that she cared for him. He would never forget how thoughtful she looked or how tenderly she had smiled at him.

The influence of Fred's mother lingered with Aunt Katy, too. The old cook was often mean after that, but no more so to Fred than to the other children. Sometimes they got smaller servings of food than they wanted, but they always got something. Still, Fred had been used to far more nourishment before he arrived than he got from Aunt Katy.

At times Fred became so hungry that he resorted to lying under the kitchen table. He had noticed that Aunt Katy often threw scraps of food there for old Nep, the dog.

Fred was too young to work in the fields, and there was little other work a child his age could do. Occasionally he did a little sweeping or brought the cows from their pasture. Otherwise, he and the other youngsters ran loose over the plantation together and explored nearby.

One of Fred's favorite spots was on Long Point, a tract of land that lay between Miles River and the River Wye. There stood an old wooden tower-type windmill which was used for draining the land. All the machinery was located in the tower, which was capped by a movable roof. At the top there were sails or wings. When the wind caught the sails, they turned the machinery.

Fred loved to watch the sails turning against a background of the sky. He enjoyed listening to the clank of the machinery as it drained the land and pumped the water into the river.

Offshore in the Wye River a large white boat sometimes anchored. She was named the *Sally Lloyd* in honor of Colonel Lloyd's daughter. The boat carried products from the plantation to market in Baltimore or Annapolis.

Occasionally, Fred went to Long Point when the time came for the *Sally Lloyd* to sail. All the crew would bustle about on deck getting ready. At last, they would haul up the white mainsail and the jib. Then up would come the anchor, and off the *Sally Lloyd* would go, her sails filled with wind.

The sight of the boat sailing away pleased Fred, but it also filled him with intense longing. What did it feel like to sail away like that, free as a bird? Would he ever know?

Chapter 5

Fred Learns
a Hard Lesson

Long Point was only one of many places where
Fred spent his playtime. Except for the formal area
close to the Great House, where he had trespassed his
first day, he explored all parts of the huge plantation.

Close to the formal area, but outside it, was a place
called "the park," where Fred sometimes went alone
to sit. He had learned that, if he was patient, he often
would be rewarded by seeing rabbits, deer, and other
wild animals.

A few of the animals would come close enough to
touch Fred. Among them was a female deer. She would
come up behind him and put her wet nose against his
neck. Occasionally she would lick him with her rough
tongue. He was always careful not to move a muscle,
because he didn't want to scare her away.

A pair of raccoons would crawl all over Fred,
digging their paws into the pocket of his shirt and

tucking their heads into the curve of his arm. Then they would sit and look at him with beady eyes from behind their black masks.

The raccoons also allowed Fred to hold and stroke them, and he was glad to have warm, living things to cuddle. He had enjoyed little cuddling in his own life, only a few rockings in his grandmother's arms, and he found it pleasant and satisfying. He didn't know yet that slaves were not supposed to have emotions—that slaveholders tried to erase their slaves' human feelings.

The other boys couldn't understand why Fred liked the park, or why he wanted to spend so much time with deer or rabbits when he could watch horses. "The stables are the place where things are going on," they said.

When Fred wanted to be where things were going on, he went to the stables, too. About thirty-five horses, all of them chosen for blood, speed, and beauty, were kept there. They were all for the use of Colonel Lloyd's household. Some were trained to pull carriages in the summer and sleighs in the winter. Some were reserved for hunting with hounds. The daintiest of all were kept for gentle riding by the ladies.

Two enslaved men were in charge of the stables, a father and son, called Old Barney and Young Barney. Colonel Lloyd allowed them to work together because of their genius as horse-handlers.

"It must be nice to have a father," Fred had said

The raccoons also allowed Fred to hold and stroke them,
and he was glad to have warm, living things to cuddle.

when he first heard of their relationship. He supposed
he himself had a father, but he didn't know who he
was. Slave children seldom knew about their fathers
and seldom had last names. Fred went by his mother's
last name, which was Bailey. She knew what her last
name was, because her parents, like the Barneys, had
been too valuable to be separated.

"The Barneys don't have it easy," Fred was told.
"You'll find out sooner or later if you stay around the
stables."

The first few times Fred went to the stables he

noticed nothing disagreeable. The harness room smelled pleasantly of leather and of the medicines Old Barney used for treating sick horses. The stalls were kept clean, strewn often with fresh straw.

The horses throughout the stable were sleek and well groomed. Young Barney was always combing the mane or brushing the tail of a horse. He made sure that each horse was well shod, with feet and legs free from blemishes.

The two Barneys lived in the stable, but Fred didn't consider that a hardship. "Even if they sleep in a stall with the horses, their beds are softer than ours are," he said to the other boys. "They sleep on that straw, whereas we sleep on bare floors. Besides, it's light and airy in the stables, a lot lighter and airier than my closet off the kitchen!"

"Just the same," the boys replied, "you've no cause to envy them. You'll see."

And one day Fred saw. In later years, he referred to the scene as "one of the most heart-saddening and humiliating" he had ever witnessed.

That forenoon Fred knelt beside Old Barney, watching him apply a poultice to a mare's lame knee. The old man's hands were gentle, and the animal stood quietly under his touch. Suddenly, there was the sound of trampling hoofs in the stable yard, and in a moment Colonel Lloyd came striding into the barn.

This was the first time Fred had ever seen the plantation owner, but he knew at once who he was. The Colonel was elegantly dressed in riding clothes, and he wore a stovepipe hat over his silver hair. His face was red with anger and he carried a riding whip loose in one hand as if threatening to use it.

"Get into the yard and take a look at that animal I've been riding!" the Colonel ordered Old Barney. "There's a twist in his reins and dust in his hair!"

The loud voice startled the mare, but Old Barney managed to keep the wet pad in place on her sore. "Didn't you hear me, you old rascal?" shouted the Colonel, snapping his whip.

"Yes, sir," said Old Barney.

Old Barney took one of Fred's hands and placed it on the poultice to hold the poultice in place. By now the mare was used to Fred and didn't mind his taking over. Fred continued to hold the wet pad in place and to speak gently to the horse.

From where he knelt, he could see through the open stable door into the yard. Colonel Lloyd had forced Old Barney onto his knees and ordered him to strip off his shirt.

Fred almost cried out in protest. Even if Old Barney was guilty of neglecting a horse, which Fred doubted, he shouldn't be treated in this manner. Then, to Fred's horror, Colonel Lloyd raised his horsewhip

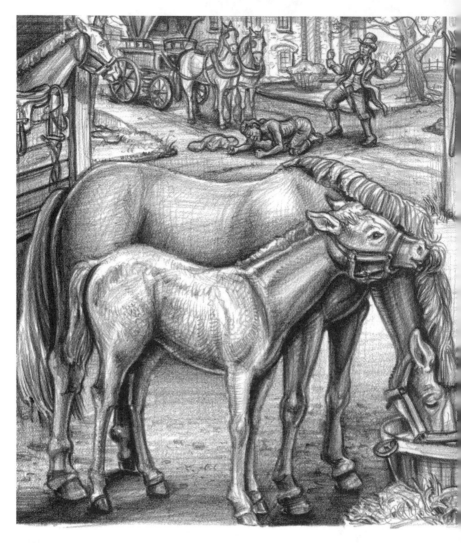

and slapped it down on Old Barney's bare shoulders.

At that, Fred gasped. The mare looked around at him curiously, but he didn't see her. He had shut his eyes tight. He couldn't help hearing what was going on in the yard, but he was determined not to watch.

After a while, the swish of the long lash stopped.

Then, to Fred's horror, Colonel Lloyd raised his horsewhip
and slapped it down on Old Barney's bare shoulders.

Fred waited a few seconds, opened his eyes again, and
saw Colonel Lloyd walk away.

Old Barney, still shirtless, was leading the Colonel's
mount toward his stall in the stable. When he reached

the stall the old slave sat down heavily on a three-legged stool.

"The mare is all right now," Old Barney said. "Do you think you can minister to me, Fred, if I tell you what to do?"

"I can try," said Fred.

Under the old man's directions, Fred mixed flour and mustard with hot water to make a smooth paste. "Now soak a piece of this rag in the soft paste and dab it over my back," Old Barney said.

Fred had avoided looking at the man's injured back, but now he had to see it. He gritted his teeth, but applied the remedy until he was told to stop.

"The mustard smarts something fierce on my back," Old Barney said, putting on his shirt, "but it will help the cuts to heal."

Just then, Young Barney came into the stable. He knew at once what had happened and he clenched his fists. "Who did it, the Colonel or one of those cowardly sons-in-law?" he asked, Old Barney kept his lips firmly closed, so Young Barney asked Fred. "The Colonel did it," Fred stammered.

"What was his excuse?"

"Twisted reins and dust," Fred said.

"Dust!" snorted Young Barney. "He'd been riding, hadn't he? Of course there was dust! Oh, if only I dared, I'd show him what dust is! Why did I have to be born a slave?"

That questioning cry rang again in Fred's ears that night as he lay sleepless for a while in his drafty little closet. Why was anybody born a slave? What gave some men the right to own other men?

Fred remembered his grandmother saying, "All things happen for a reason. There is a purpose for everything. It isn't up to us to question why things happen the way they do."

Until Fred had seen Old Barney whipped, he had accepted his grandmother's explanation.

Now he couldn't accept it any longer. How could it be good for Old Barney to be whipped when he hadn't done anything wrong?

From this experience, Fred learned that in a slave society such as his, the whip was all-important. Slaveholders used the whip to punish disobedience and maintain control. Slaves in positions of authority did the same with children or other slaves with less authority.

Chapter 6

A Little Bit
of Kindness

Kindness and patience were the exception, not the rule, on Colonel Lloyd's plantation. Luckily for Fred, he saw both displayed regularly by Old Barney at the stables. He practiced them himself with wild animals. Otherwise, he might have become hard-hearted himself.

As the months passed, Fred was forced to witness other beatings besides that of Old Barney. Each time he wanted to help the victim, but he knew that he couldn't do anything alone. "It would be like one chicken against a fox," he thought. "Now if there were lots of chickens, things would be different."

And one day, there were. Fred was returning from the river where he recently had learned to dig oysters and to eat them raw.

Suddenly, Fred heard screams and curses. A female slave named Nelly was being dragged toward a tree by the overseer, Mr. Sevier. Evidently he planned to tie her to the tree and whip her. "I'll teach you to talk back to me," he yelled.

Nelly was not as meek as many slaves. She probably had dared to stick up for herself when the overseer had accused her of something. But right or wrong, saying anything at all was considered to be impudence. Slaves weren't permitted to defend themselves. Fred had learned this, too, from Old Barney.

Nelly knew she could not escape punishment. Unlike Old Barney, however, she wasn't going to make it easy for her accuser. She started to kick and scratch.

Suddenly three of Nelly's five children came running up. "Let our mother go!" they yelled.

To Fred's delight, two of the children, who were boys, began to pelt the overseer with stones. The third, a little girl, seized hold of his leg and started to bite him.

Fred's heart gave a great leap. Here was his chance to hit back! In his pocket he had half a dozen sharp-edged oyster shells which he had saved to use as food scoops.

One after the other, Fred aimed the shells at the overseer's face. Some brought blood, and Fred was glad. "We can't save Nelly from getting a whipping," he exulted, "but we can make Mr. Sevier sorry he picked on her!"

Fred was now being given more tasks to do, so he needed to learn how to deal with the owners and overseers. He was expected to perform small tasks for his master's daughter, Miss Lucretia. She had recently married and returned to live in her father's house with her husband, Thomas Auld.

Fred was happy to serve Miss Lucretia. Before her marriage, she had sometimes noticed him when she came to the kitchen to talk to Aunt Katy about household matters. She had smiled at him from time to time and patted him on the head. Once she had even given him a cookie hot from the oven. He remembered this kindness.

The things she asked him to do were easy. On hot days, he waved a palm-leaf fan to cool her. On cool days, he brought her foot-warming bricks, which were kept always ready on the back of the wood stove in the kitchen for just that purpose. Sometimes he held her horse's bridle while she mounted, or gave her a "hand up" as she stepped into her carriage.

Fred made a habit of playing under Miss Lucretia's window, so he'd be ready when she called. One day, while he was playing there, he sang a tune he'd learned from an enslaved man on one of Colonel Lloyd's ships. He liked the repetition of the word "sail", and he had memorized the song quickly.

Fred's heart gave a great leap.
Here was his chance to hit back!

"Sail, O believer, sail,
Sail over yonder,
Sail, O my brother, sail,
Sail over yonder."

Miss Lucretia heard Fred singing. She leaned out the window. "I didn't know you could sing, Fred," she said. "Do you know any more songs like that one?"

Fred shook his head. "No, ma'am," he replied, "only more of the same one." Then he sang the second verse.

"Come view the promised land,
Sail over yonder.
O brother lend a hand,
Sail over yonder!"

Miss Lucretia clapped her hands. "For singing that song, you deserve a reward," she said.

"Stay where you are and I'll be back in a jiffy."

Soon Miss Lucretia returned and handed him a thick slice of white bread spread with brown sugar. His eyes shone and his mouth began to water as he took the bread.

"Eat, child, eat," Miss Lucretia said.

Fred began to eat, but he took very small bites. He wanted to make his reward last as long as possible.

After that, Fred listened closely to the songs the slaves sang. They often sang as they worked, because the overseer didn't like silent people. "Make a noise! Make a noise!" he'd shout, and crack his whip threateningly.

The slaveholders didn't know that the songs which slaves sang often had double meanings.

Neither, of course, did Fred at his young age, but he realized it before he was many years older. Every word in a song was a testimony against slavery. Every verse expressed a yearning to be free.

From this time on, Miss Lucretia favored Fred, and Aunt Katy resented his good luck. She was jealous because she had children of her own. Consequently, she often slapped Fred and accused him of all manner of things. She remembered his mother's threats, however, and continued to feed him with the other children.

Aunt Katy didn't care what happened to Fred when he was out of her sight. One day, a much older boy fought him with a sharp piece of cinder fused with iron from the blacksmith's forge.

He received a number of long scratches and a severe gash on his forehead. The gash began to bleed freely, and the sight of the blood frightened him. He began to cry and ran back to the kitchen seeking help.

"Serves you right," Aunt Katy said, making no

effort to stop the bleeding or his crying.

Her callousness made Fred cry even louder. Miss Lucretia heard him and came hurrying to see what was the matter. "Oh, poor child!" she said, shocked.

She led Fred into Old Master's parlor and had him lie down on the horsehair sofa. Then she brought water and soft cloths, with which she washed and bound up his wounds. "There, now you'll soon be fine," she said, "but lie there until you feel better."

Fred felt better at once, but wasn't ready to admit it yet. He'd never been in Old Master's parlor before, and he might never be there again. He wanted to stay as long as he could.

Miss Lucretia went to the side of the room and started to play a melodeon, a kind of piano. Fred listened, surprised and entranced, for a little while. He felt very peaceful and comfortable, so comfortable that he fell asleep.

Chapter 7

Fred Takes a Trip

When Fred awoke, he heard voices murmuring behind him. He turned over and saw Miss Lucretia talking to Old Master. He stayed quiet.

Fred heard his name, but he was being talked about, not to. He shut his eyes, pretending he was still asleep. He wanted to listen to find out what was happening.

"Somehow you think Katy can do no wrong," Fred heard Miss Lucretia say to her father, "but you are mistaken. She's a regular devil in the way she treats this poor child."

"Nonsense!" sputtered Captain Anthony. "It doesn't do to coddle little slave children. It just spoils them for the future."

"That may be," Miss Lucretia answered, "but you didn't see what I saw today."

There was silence for a moment. Fred lay very still. He knew that Miss Lucretia and her father might be looking in his direction. "Well," Captain Anthony said, "he's your boy. If you want to send him to Thomas's brother, I won't stop you."

At these words, Fred's heart beat so hard he was afraid they could hear it, but they didn't.

Soon Captain Anthony left, and Miss Lucretia called softly, "Fred, wake up."

For another few heartbeats, Fred made no response. Miss Lucretia put a hand on his shoulder and shook him gently. This time Fred opened his eyes. He would have sat up, but Miss Lucretia held him back.

"Move slowly," she said, "so you don't start the bleeding again." She helped him gradually to a sitting position, then looked him over critically. "You're dirty," she said.

Fred said nothing. He looked no different than he always did. She just hadn't noticed before. "Well, you'll have to scrub yourself clean," she continued. "Miss Sophy wouldn't want you near Tommy, otherwise."

These names meant nothing to Fred, but if Miss Lucretia wanted him to scrub himself clean, he would. He stood up, ready to start the hard scrubbing.

Miss Lucretia laughed. "Aren't you going to ask why?" she asked.

"No, ma'am," said Fred. He had often been told that slaves were wise only to say yes or no to white people. Otherwise, they might get a whipping for being familiar.

Miss Lucretia laughed again. "I'm going to tell you anyway. You are going to Baltimore to live with Mr. and Mrs. Hugh Auld. Mr. Auld is my husband's brother. He wants a trustworthy boy to look after his son Tommy."

Fred forgot his lesson about not talking. "Baltimore!" he cried. "I'm going?"

"Yes, you," Miss Lucretia replied. "You're going Saturday." She looked at him closely again.

"You'll have to have some other clothes," she added. "You'll need a clean shirt, and, for goodness sake, a pair of trousers."

The thought of owning trousers was almost as exciting to Fred as going to Baltimore. Slaves weren't issued trousers until they became field hands or house servants. If he was going to look after a boy named Tommy, he probably would be a house servant. What luck!

As soon as Miss Lucretia let him go, Fred made a beeline for the creek. He and the other children had often waded in the creek but had never bathed in it. They were too afraid of getting a licking from Aunt Katy for getting their clothes wet. This time, however, Fred sat down boldly. He grabbed a handful of sand and began to scour himself.

Fred spent much of the next two days in the creek,

scrubbing himself almost raw. On Friday evening, he felt that he was ready for inspection. He took his usual place under Miss Lucretia's window and began to sing.

"I built my house upon the rock,
O yes!"

Miss Lucretia had evidently been expecting him, for she came out at once. "Let me look at you," she said.

She gave special attention to Fred's knees and feet, which had been particularly encrusted with dirt. Fred waited anxiously for her decision. Would he pass her careful inspection?

Miss Lucretia smiled and patted him on the head. "Stay here just a minute," she said, "while I go to get your new clothes."

The new clothing included a shirt such as Fred had been wearing for years, linen trousers, and a pair of coarse shoes. The last two items brought joy to Fred's heart because he had never possessed either before. "Oh, thank you!" he cried, clutching them to his breast.

Pity, or some similar emotion, brought tears to Miss Lucretia's eyes. She smoothed the mound of clothes and said, "Remember to wash once you get to

Baltimore, Fred. I don't want Mr. Hugh Auld to be sorry we sent you."

Fred didn't sleep much that night. He was to go by ship, which would sail at sunup the next morning, and he was afraid he'd be left behind.

He didn't mind his sleeplessness, however, because he had so much to think about. Fred had no regrets about leaving the home place. It had never been home to him the way his grandmother's cabin in Tuckahoe had been. Except for Miss Lucretia, nobody here cared anything for him. His brothers and sisters would soon be sent away, and he had been told recently that his mother had died.

Baltimore at least would be different. He had heard about the city from the boatman who had taught him the "Sail Over Yonder" song. One boatman, who was a cousin of his, had said that nothing Fred had ever seen could compare with Baltimore.

"Why, there are ships there that could carry four such sloops as Colonel Lloyd owns," he had boasted. "And some houses there would make Lloyd's Great House look very small."

Now Fred was not only going to see it, he was going to live there. Even if he had to endure whippings in his new home, they could be no worse than whippings he would have had to endure on Colonel Lloyd's plantation.

Fred went aboard the sloop before dawn. A deckhand called Rich guided him to a place by the rail. "Stay here until it's light enough to see what you're doing," he said. "After that, just keep out of the way!"

Fred clutched the railing with trembling hands. It was exciting to be on a boat for the first time! Soon he'd be sailing down the river out into the bay. And he'd be free as a bird, at least until he reached Baltimore.

As soon as it was light, Fred walked to the stern of the sloop. He took what he hoped was his last look at Colonel Lloyd's plantation. Then, careful not to get in the path of the bustling deck-hands, he went to the bow. Here he could look ahead to see where the sloop was going.

Fred spent most of the day looking out across the water. The broad bay seemed to be alive with ships of all kinds. Some had colored sails and others white sails. Fred liked white sails best, like those on his own vessel, because they looked like clouds against the blue sky.

Late in the afternoon, the sloop docked briefly at Annapolis, the capital of the state of Maryland. Fred gazed in wonder, because it was the first large town he had ever seen. He wondered whether Baltimore would be as large and grand as Annapolis.

Rich came to lean over the railing and look with him. "This is a big place," he said.

Fred spent most of the day looking out across the water.
The broad bay seemed to be alive with ships of all kinds.

"Yes. Is Baltimore as large and grand as this?"
asked Fred.

"Well, it's larger, maybe fifty times larger," said
Rich, "but I don't know about it being any grander
than Annapolis."

Fred gasped. He couldn't even imagine a place that big. "What keeps a person from getting lost there, maybe on purpose?" he asked.

"By person, do you mean a slave?" Rich asked. "If you mean a slave, you would find it very hard to get lost."

"Why?" asked Fred.

"Because of the Fugitive Slave Law, that's why," replied Rich.

Fred had never heard of this law. "What's that?" he asked.

"I don't know what it says, but it lets slave owners hunt down runaway slaves, just like foxes. Have you ever seen a fox brought back by hounds?"

Fred shuddered. He had seen this once or twice, and hoped he'd never see it again. Just then a whistle turned their minds from the sickening subject of foxes and hounds. It was time for Rich to get to work. The ship was going to get under way again.

"Wait for me here when we get to Baltimore," Rich said. "Then I'll help you find the place where you are supposed to go."

Darkness was beginning to fall as the sloop moved away from the dock. Lights appeared in the town a few at a time, reminding Fred of the fireflies he'd chased when he was smaller.

When night had completely fallen, Fred suddenly

Darkness was beginning to fall as the sloop
moved away from the dock.

realized he was hungry. He hadn't eaten since morning, when he'd had his usual meager meal of mush.
When he had left, Aunt Katy had handed him something wrapped in corn husks. "Miss Lucretia told me
to give you this," she said.

Fred had wedged the package into a little space he
had found under the railing. "Hurrah" he exclaimed
when he unwrapped the package and saw two thick
slices of corn bread with a chunk of salt pork between
them. This generous meal, he knew, was due to Miss
Lucretia's insistence, not Aunt Katy's generosity.

After he had eaten, he lay down on the deck. "Now
if only Miss Sophy could be as nice to young slave boys
as Miss Lucretia. . ." he murmured drowsily.

Chapter 8

A Child Like
Any Other

The sloop tied up at Smith's wharf in Baltimore early Sunday morning. Fred heard bells ringing and many dockside sounds, including the bleating of sheep. Many sheep were being herded down a ramp to shore.

"I have to help drive the sheep to the slaughter-house," said Rich, suddenly appearing at Fred's side. "Come along and we'll go from there to Auld's place."

Fred had helped to herd cows from the pasture to the barn on the plantation, but he'd never handled sheep before. He saw little of the surroundings through which he walked, because he was busy watching the sheep. After they were safely penned, he started off with Rich for Alliciana Street.

"What are Mr. and Mrs. Hugh Auld like?" he asked, for he knew that Rich had frequently been sent on errands to the Auld home.

Rich shrugged his shoulders. "They are all right, I guess," he said. "Miss Sophy once gave me a drink of water out of a glass."

When they reached the Auld house, Fred was highly pleased with their reception. The owners, Mr. and Mrs. Auld, were at the front door to meet them. Behind his mother, clinging to her skirts, was little Tommy.

"Welcome to Baltimore, Fred," Mr. Auld said. "Rich, thank you for bringing him."

Rich would have left right away, but Mrs. Auld stopped him. "The cook will give you some food, Rich," she said. "You know where to go."

After Rich left for the kitchen, Mrs. Auld drew Tommy out from behind her. "Tommy, this is Freddy," she said, putting Tommy's chubby little hand into Fred's lean brown hand. "Freddy will help to take care of you and be kind to you. Won't you, Fred?"

Fred, holding Tommy's hand, was all but tongue-tied by this pleasing statement. "Yes, ma'am," he managed to say.

Mrs. Auld smiled and said, "Now we'll show you where you are to sleep, so you'll begin to feel at home."

She led the way through the hallway and up carpeted stairs to a little room. "This will be your room here, Fred," she said. "Tommy's room is next door."

Fred, hesitating on the threshold, could scarcely believe his eyes. He saw a bright, clean room with a window! A real bedstead and real covers! And there was a chest of drawers and a stand with a bowl and pitcher.

Mrs. Auld gave Fred a little push. "You may use the water in the pitcher to wash your hands and face," she said. "Tommy and I will go to his room. Then you may come there."

Fred poured water into the bowl and washed his face and hands. Then he walked slowly around the room, touching everything. He sat briefly on the bed, which was soft like the sofa in Captain Anthony's parlor. He opened drawers and discovered special clothes intended for him.

Neither Hugh nor Sophia Auld had ever had a slave before, and both treated him like any other child. If Tommy got a treat, so did Fred. He was accepted, in fact, as a member of the family.

Naturally, in this atmosphere, Fred's behavior changed, too. Instead of speaking to these white folks in as few words as possible, he really talked with them. And he dared to look at them as he spoke without fearing they would think he was impudent.

Hugh Auld was a shipbuilder. Shortly after Fred's arrival, he got some new contracts which required him to spend more and more time away from home. One day Fred overheard him ask his wife, "Do you think you can manage Fred alone, my dear?"

"Yes, I certainly can," she replied. "After all, he is only nine years old."

"Well," said Hugh, not sounding too sure, "keep him busy. I've heard that idle slaves often become troublemakers."

Fred held his breath for a few seconds, waiting for Mrs. Auld's reply. "He's only a child," she said.

Fred let out his breath again with a sigh of relief. Mrs. Auld really was different from anybody he had ever known before.

Mrs. Auld managed to keep Fred busy watching five-year-old Tommy. He held Tommy's hand when they walked to the playground. He took a tight grip on the child's clothing to keep him from falling into the duck pond. He acted like a responsible big brother.

As the months went by, Fred grew more and more accustomed to kind treatment instead of abuse. When Mrs. Auld held Tommy on her knee, she encouraged Fred to sit on a footstool close by. Often she read aloud to both boys from the Bible.

Fred had never heard anyone read before. He was fascinated by the book which told Mrs. Auld what words to say. One day, he chanced to be alone in the room where the Bible was. Hesitantly he opened the book and stared at the rows and rows of black print. How did they tell Mrs. Auld what to say?

Mrs. Auld entered the room and saw Fred looking at the open book. "What are you doing, Fred?" she asked.

Fred, taken by surprise, started. "No harm, I hope," he said quickly.

Mrs. Auld smiled. "Perhaps I should have asked, 'What are you trying to do?'"

"To find out how you know what words to say," Fred answered. "I'd like to say them, too."

Mrs. Auld looked pleased. "You mean you'd like to learn how to read, Fred? How wonderful! We'll begin at once."

She kept her word, using the family Bible as Fred's textbook. First she pointed out a small "a" and a large "A" and said them aloud. Fred looked and repeated after her. Then she turned a page and had him find both the small and large letters for himself. After he had proved that he knew them, she went on to the "b's" and the "c's," "d's," and "e's" before she stopped the lesson for the day. "You're a very good pupil, Fred," she said with a smile.

Fred didn't know what that meant, but he could tell she was pleased with him. "Tomorrow we'll continue," she promised.

Learning a few letters at a time, Fred soon became

master of the printed alphabet. Shortly he could read and spell words of three or four letters. "You'll soon be reading the Bible for yourself," Mrs. Auld said.

The next day Hugh Auld came home unexpectedly and found Mrs. Auld giving Fred his lesson. "Sophia, what do you think you're doing?" he almost shouted.

"Teaching Fred to read," she replied simply. "He's a very apt pupil."

"Well, stop teaching him at once!" Mr. Auld commanded rather sharply. "It's unsafe to teach a slave to read."

"Why!" she asked, shocked. "How can it be unsafe for anybody to read the Bible?"

"Well, it would be all right if he would be content just to read the Bible, but he wouldn't," Hugh Auld continued. "The first thing you know, he'll be reading anti-slavery literature. Then who knows what he'd do? We might not even be safe in his company."

Fred heard Hugh Auld's words with a sinking heart because he knew that they were bound to influence Mrs. Auld. As he thought about them later, however, he realized that they helped him to understand what made some people slaves and some people free. The secret was simply this—knowledge, or the lack of it, made the difference.

"Sometime, when I know enough, I'll know how to gain my freedom," Fred said to himself. "And when

"Well, stop teaching him at once!" Mr. Auld commanded rather sharply. "It's unsafe to teach a slave to read."

that day comes I'll really be free!"

Without knowing it, Hugh Auld had done Fred a great service. He had set his feet on the long pathway that led from slavery to eventual freedom.

Chapter 9

A Giant Step

After Hugh Auld objected to his wife teaching Fred to read, she did an abrupt about-face. She not only stopped trying to teach Fred, but also tried to keep him away from things to read. However, Fred was determined to continue his education, although at the moment he did not know how.

From time to time as Fred had run errands for Mrs. Auld, he had met white boys running errands for their parents. Occasionally they had played a game together, such as playing marbles, spinning tops, or broad jumping. Afterwards, they had sat on the curb to rest and had talked about things that concerned them. Bit by bit Fred had told them what it was like to be enslaved.

Quite naturally, he told the boys his sad tale the next time he saw them. They found it hard to believe, because in Baltimore most slaves were well treated. "That wasn't fair," one of the boys declared.

"It must be illegal!" said another.

"I wouldn't stand for it," said a third, "but I guess you'll have to."

All the boys sat thinking and talking for a few moments. Finally a fourth boy said, "I know what we can do, Fred. *We* can teach you."

That idea pleased everybody. The boys at once got Fred a dog-eared copy of Webster's spelling book. They brought him their papers from school and scraps of newspaper. From then on, whenever Fred and his friends met on the street, they didn't waste time playing games. They played school instead.

One day, about three years after Fred had come to Baltimore, something happened that was far more unsettling than Hugh Auld's unfairness. Through the years he had learned that he belonged to the "Old Master," Captain Anthony. In the summer of 1829, when Captain Anthony died, Fred became part of the property that had to be divided between Captain Anthony's children, Andrew and Lucretia. He had to return to the plantation to be valued and reassigned.

The state of affairs greatly distressed Mrs. Auld and her son, Tommy. She had come to think of Fred almost as a son, and Tommy had come to think of him as a brother. All three shed tears when they had to say good-bye. Fred knew that he might not return.

Fred still knew that he was enslaved, but he had

become used to being treated like a human being. So he was shocked when he returned to the plantation and was shut into a pen with dozens of other slaves, including men, women, and children of all ages and conditions of health.

Alongside this pen were other pens, some bigger, some smaller, which contained horses, sheep, cattle and pigs. Both people and animals, Fred learned, had to be closely examined to determine their value. Their arms and legs were pinched, their teeth inspected, their eyes and ears tested for soundness. Each was then tagged to show what he was supposed to be worth.

At first, Fred felt very low in spirits. He knew that he wouldn't be considered of very high value. He was only twelve years old, too young to work in the fields. And he wondered what use he could be to either the Thomas Aulds or to Andrew Anthony.

He also heard dreadful things about Master Andrew. Most of the other slaves had a horror of falling into his hands. He had a bad disposition and besides was often short of money. When this happened, he would sell anything he owned at public auction.

Eventually, the prodding and pinching and tallying were over. To Fred's sobbing relief, he was allotted to Lucretia Auld. For a short while, he stayed with the Thomas Aulds, but was then sent back to Baltimore.

His reunion with the Baltimore Aulds was joyous. Miss Sophy hugged him and cried. Tommy capered about like an organ grinder's monkey. Even Master Hugh clapped his shoulder and said, "Welcome home."

For the rest of the summer, Fred felt completely happy. He resumed his care of Tommy and took him daily to the park to play. He did small chores about the yard, such as scrubbing the white steps, clipping the grass, and burning the trash.

When fall came, Tommy started school, and Fred had a new task. For a while he had to escort Tommy back and forth morning and evening. Seeing Tommy go in the school, where he was not allowed, felt like a very bitter punishment.

Fred began to think more and more about the sadness of slavery. Sometimes he saw Mrs. Auld looking at him with a puzzled expression. He longed to tell her that she had started much of his misery. If she had never begun to teach him how to read, he wouldn't know what he was missing. Instead, he would have been just as happy as her little dog, and just as dumb.

He seldom got a chance now to talk with the local boys as he had before, but one time he did manage to talk with them. Though they had no chance to teach him anything, they told him about a book called *The*

Both people and animals, Fred learned, had to be closely
examined to determine their value.

Columbian Orator, which they read in school. "We
have to learn pieces from it to say out loud," one boy
told him one afternoon.

"It's great!" said another. "It includes speeches
by Patrick Henry and William Pitt and all kinds of
famous people."

"You really ought to get a copy," said a third boy. "It
even includes parts about slaves and freeing them."

"You can buy one at Mr. Knight's shop on Thames
Street," volunteered a fourth boy.

As soon as Fred could, he made his way to Thames
Street. Mr. Knight saw him peering wistfully into the

window and came out to talk to him. "What do you want, boy?" he asked, in such a kindly voice that Fred felt he could tell him what he wanted.

Fortunately, Mr. Knight kept no slaves and did not approve of anybody else keeping them. He did not believe in keeping slaves ignorant either. "Do fifty cents' worth of work for me and you may have the book," he said.

So Fred obtained the book which the boys had recommended. This took him another big step along the road to freedom.

Chapter 10

Fred Gets Ideas

Fred read the new book thoughtfully page by page and found it very comforting. It introduced him to the ideas that Hugh Auld had been afraid he would discover. It taught him that men were willing to die rather than be enslaved. It showed him that many believed "all men were created equal."

The next time Fred saw his white friends he told them how he felt. "That book you told me to read!" he cried. "It says that nobody was born to be a slave!"

"We told you that we didn't think it was right for us to be free and you not to be free," they reminded him.

"Yes, but I didn't know any grown folks felt that way," replied Fred.

"Many grown folks do," the boys explained. "Some of them, called abolitionists, are starting to do something about it."

"Ab-o-lition-ists," Fred repeated slowly. He remembered that he had heard the word spoken by Hugh Auld and his guests. Not knowing what it meant, he hadn't paid any attention. From now on, he would listen more closely.

Fred snatched every chance to be useful to Hugh Auld when company was around. He moved about the room serving delicacies to the visitors or fanning them when they were overheated. He was so constantly present that guests paid no more attention to him than they paid to what he served.

One evening, Fred heard the word "abolitionist" repeated and repeated with increasing anger and bitterness. "The abolitionists are out to ruin us slaveholders," one guest declared.

"Yes, they would just as soon burn our houses with us in them," said another.

"They don't seem to realize that most of us treat our slaves exactly as we treat our children," Hugh Auld said.

At that, quite unconsciously, Fred shook his head, causing him to jiggle the bottles on a tray. The sound drew Hugh Auld's attention. "Watch what you're doing, boy!" he said.

"Yes, sir," said Fred.

His answer was polite enough, but something in the tone of his voice or his posture disturbed Mr. Auld. "We won't need you anymore tonight," he said. "Take the tray back to the kitchen and go to bed."

Fred had no choice but to obey.

After that evening, Fred heard no more talk of abolition when he was near. This made him sure it was something he wasn't supposed to know about. His curiosity increased.

One day, Mr. Auld carelessly left a copy of the *Baltimore American* lying about. Fred, eager for anything new to read, took the paper and hid it behind the drapery.

It proved to be a gold mine of information about abolitionists. It talked of a movement to abolish slavery in the District of Columbia. It spoke of a law to prevent slave trade between the states. Most important of all, it helped Fred to discover that there were states where no slavery existed.

This news put new hope into his heart. If the abolitionists became strong enough, maybe they could abolish slavery in Maryland someday.

The question was, where could he find people who shared these ideas? Fortunately, Hugh Auld again played into Fred's hands. He decided that Tommy was able to walk to and from school now and that Fred could spend his time helping out at the shipyard. He would do odd jobs that didn't require skill.

At the shipyard, Fred now had a chance to talk to all sorts of people. Among them was an old man, known as Uncle Lawson.

After Fred had known Uncle Lawson for a short

time, the old man invited him to come to a meeting at the Bethel Church. At this meeting, Fred found people he had been seeking, people like himself who shared his ideas about slavery.

Fred managed to attend a number of meetings before Mr. Auld found out about them. "I forbid you to go there again!" he said. "If you do, I'll have to whip you."

One day at noon, when Fred was idling on the wharf, he saw two white men laboring to unload a scow. He offered to help them and afterwards they thanked him. "That was a very kind thing to do," they said.

"I was glad to help," Fred said.

The men looked at him curiously. "Are you a slave or a bound boy?" they asked.

A bound boy, Fred knew, was a boy bound to serve a master for only a limited time, but he didn't know any black person who was that lucky. "I'm a slave, bound for life," he said.

"That's too bad for a nice upstanding young fellow like you," said one of the men.

"Why don't you run away?" asked the other.

"Go north, to Pennsylvania, a free state, and you'll likely find people to help you."

The thought of running away had never occurred to Fred. It was a new idea, but he might do it someday.

His heart leaped with excitement.

"Of course, you'd have to carry papers saying you had a right to be where you are," the first man warned. "You'd have to be careful about talking with people, too."

Fred suddenly realized Mr. Auld wouldn't approve of his talking with strange white men. Besides, how did he know he could trust the men not to report what he said to Mr. Auld? He swallowed hard and replied, "I have a good master and mistress. Why should I run away?"

The men exchanged glances and shrugged.

"Suit yourself," one of them said.

"Yes, go on being a slave," said the other.

The men turned their backs on Fred. He hesitated a moment, then walked slowly away from them. He was sorry to hurt them, if they were being kind, but how could he know?

Fred liked working at the now familiar shipyard. He liked the clean smell of sawdust and the sharp scent of the pine tar used to fill holes. He liked to hear the rhythm of saws and the steady pounding of nails.

One day, he noticed that the carpenters marked each piece of cut timber with a letter. After watching them awhile, he asked why they did this.

The carpenters seemed happy to explain. "On a piece ready for the starboard side, we write 's,' and for the larboard side we write 'l.' For larboard forward we write 'l.f.' and for larboard aft, 'l.a.' Get it?"

Fred nodded. So this was writing! All he had ever seen was printing. Now he wanted to learn to write. "I'll teach myself," he decided. "Any educated person has to know how."

At first, he was at a loss for writing materials. Then he remembered his grandmother's calendar. She had used a sharp stick to make marks in the damp earth. He could do the same.

Eagerly, he copied "a's," "f's," "s's," and "l's" until he could write them easily. As soon as he had a chance, he showed his white friends what he could do.

"Good for you," they said. "Now you'll have to learn all the other letters."

Fred's face fell. The carpenters didn't use any other letters that he knew about.

"We'll teach you," his friends offered.

Fred realized it wouldn't be safe to practice writing all the letters in the earth of the shipyard. He would have to find some other way to practice.

What he found were copybooks which Tommy had used in school. He took these to his own room and hid them. Only at night, after everyone else was in bed, did he dare get them out and practice.

The first long piece he copied was Patrick Henry's famous speech before the Virginia Convention. Afterwards, he reread it proudly, lingering on the

Fred nodded. So this was writing! All he had ever seen
was printing. Now he wanted to learn to write.

ending. Somehow those strong, final words, "Give me Liberty, or give me Death!" expressed his feelings exactly.

Chapter 11

A Stubborn Mule
Needs Gentling

Six months after Fred had returned to Baltimore, Miss Lucretia died. He felt very sad on hearing the news because she had always been good to him. Also, he felt uneasy because he now belonged to her husband, Thomas Auld. For two years, however, Mr. Auld had given no sign of wanting him, and Fred had almost forgotten that he might.

But one day, Mr. Auld did. He had married Rowena Hamilton, the daughter of an aristocratic slave owner. They lived near St. Michaels, a fishing village, where they entertained many friends. Soon she heard how well Miss Lucretia had liked Fred and was determined to have him in her own household. Thomas picked a quarrel with his brother and demanded the return of his property.

Fred dreaded the thought of leaving Baltimore, but more because of the friends he had made than because he would miss the Aulds. Most of the time recently he had spent away from the Auld home. Master Hugh had hired him out to do odd jobs for other people and often he had stayed where he worked. In this way, for the first time in his life, he had come to make many friends.

The fact that he had no choice made him feel very bitter. Once on board the sloop that was taking him to St. Michaels, he clenched his fists and pounded the railing in desperation. What a fool he had been not to have run away when he had a chance! Now he was going to a place from which escape would be very difficult.

Fred had never really known Thomas Auld as the husband of gentle Miss Lucretia. He soon got to know him now, however, as the husband of haughty Miss Rowena. As a pair, they were difficult to please.

The thing that bothered Fred most about the Thomas Aulds was their stinginess with food. Their slaves were allowed even less per week than on Colonel Lloyd's plantation. Usually their ration was half a peck of corn meal per person per week, barely enough to keep them alive.

As a result, all the slaves were forced to beg or steal food. Fred soon found a prize source of food in the kitchen of Miss Rowena's father, who lived nearby.

Fred made this discovery one day by accident when he forgot to shut the barn door. Master Thomas's horse disappeared, and it was up to Fred to find the missing animal. Fortunately, he was able to follow the hoof prints of the horse, which led to the stable where the horse had formerly been kept. When he started to get the horse, Aunt Mary, the cook, called to him. "Let the horse stay for a spell. I'm baking some tarts. Come have some."

Fred ate like a starving boy, and Aunt Mary clucked over him like a mother hen. When he left, she gave him a basket of food, which he shared with the others. By careful planning, they made it last several days.

After that, Fred deliberately neglected to shut the barn door to let the horse run away. Then he went after the horse and Aunt Mary gave him some food. He kept doing this even though Thomas Auld whipped him severely for his carelessness.

Finally Auld realized Fred was deliberately letting the horse run away. "My whipping you hasn't done a bit of good," he said. "You have to be broken of your bad conduct. I've decided to lend you to Edward Covey for a year. Then we'll see whether you're ready to toe the line or not!"

Fred had already heard of Edward Covey, who had the reputation of being a first-rate hand at breaking the spirit of young enslaved men. Any master who could not control a young slave sent him to Covey. In exchange for conquering the young offender, Covey got free use of his services.

Fred went to Covey's on January 1, 1834. In spite of his dread of what lay ahead, he walked quickly. It was a bitter cold day, and his clothing was very thin. Before he reached the end of his journey, he was chilled through.

Thomas Auld had told Covey nothing about Fred except that he was "stubborn as a mule and needed gentling." Covey didn't bother to ask Fred what he was trained to do. He simply gave orders and expected them to be carried out promptly. His penalty for awkwardness or slowness was repeated use of the whip.

For the first time in his life, Fred worked as a field hand. Since he had never done field work before, he was rather awkward and slow. Besides, as soon as he learned to do one thing well, he was told to do something else. As a result, he often heard the snap of the whip and felt it on his back. For six months, scarcely a day went by without his being whipped at least once.

Finally, on a sweltering day in August, Fred and three other men were at work in the treading yard. Here, wheat was trodden out of the straw by horses.

The job was a four-part job, and each part depended on the other. The first man guided the horses. The second man gathered up the trodden wheat, and the third man fed it into a fan that blew the husks from the grain. The fourth man then measured the grain.

Thomas Auld had told Covey nothing about Fred except that he was "stubborn as a mule and needed gentling."

Fred was given the job of gathering up the trodden wheat, the hardest, hottest job of all. He worked mechanically for hours, from sunup to midafternoon. At last he became so exhausted and dizzy that he fell to the ground.

As soon as Fred collapsed, the chain of work stopped. Only the horses' feet kept moving. Up at the house, Covey missed the whirr of the fan. He came racing to see what was wrong. "Fred is sick," he was told.

"Is he?" snorted Covey. Then he looked at Fred lying on the ground and cried, "Get up!"

Fred tried, but he couldn't stand up. By now Covey was furious. "I'll teach you what it means to be sick!" he yelled.

He took the iron bucket in which Fred had been carrying wheat and beat him savagely on the head. Only when Fred fainted completely away did he stop.

Fred lay where he was until dark. Then he took off for the woods instead of dragging himself up to the house. There Sandy, from a neighboring farm, found him.

Sandy listened to Fred's story with horror and said, "Come with me. I'm on my way to visit my wife. She's a free woman and has a hut not far from here."

Sandy's wife bathed Fred's wounds and bandaged them. She gave him something to eat. Then Fred asked Sandy's advice. "Should I go back to Covey's or try to escape?"

"It's almost impossible to escape from here," Sandy said. "We live on a neck of land surrounded by water. The only road out passes St. Michaels, where everybody knows you."

"I know, but if I go back to Covey, he will kill me," Fred said.

"No, he won't, if you do what I say," Sandy told him. "I was born in Africa and learned this trick from the tribal medicine man. There is a certain root which, if worn, protects its wearer from harm. I'll get you one."

"All right," Fred said, at last, "I'll take your advice and carry a root."

Sandy gave Fred the root. Then he said, "Go back to Covey's. Walk up bravely to the house as if nothing had happened."

Fred followed this advice, and Covey didn't lift a finger against him. Fred was flabbergasted. Could the root be magic after all? Then he laughed at himself. It was now Sunday, the day Covey treated as a day of rest. That included rest from all activity, even whipping.

Fred thought hard and made up his mind. He would do exactly as Covey said, as well as he possibly could. Then, if Covey tried to beat him anyway, he'd defend himself.

"I'll show Covey that I'm a man just as he is," Fred vowed. "He has beaten me unjustly for the last time."

The next time Covey started to hit Fred, he resisted. When Covey kept on, he gave Covey blow for blow. His aim was not to injure Covey but to keep Covey from injuring him.

After a while, Covey gave up. In the six months remaining of Fred's year of service, he never tried to beat Fred again.

Chapter 12

Fred Turns Teacher

Fred returned to Thomas Auld's on Christmas Day, 1834. He expected to go back to the same chores he had before he was sent to Covey's. His master, however, had other plans, and soon sent him out on loan to another neighbor, William Freeland.

The boy who walked to Mr. Freeland's was a different boy from the one who had walked to Covey's the year before. He was larger and stronger, and he was determined never to submit to inhuman treatment again.

He soon discovered at Freeland's that he would not be treated harshly. Mr. Freeland treated his slaves like people, not animals. He gave them plenty to eat and plenty of time for eating. He worked them hard during the day, but gave them full nights of rest. He even supplied them with good tools.

If Fred had been a typical slave, he might have been contented at Freeland's. But he remembered his last months in Baltimore. There he had been able to talk with people who knew about things besides crops and cattle.

Fortunately, he found companionship in his two books, the Bible and the *Columbian Orator*. Now that he had time, he could read them again. He carried one of them inside his shirt when he went to the fields. Then during his break for lunch he refreshed himself by reading.

Before long the other men became curious about Fred and his book. They had never known an enslaved man who could read. "Is it hard to learn how to read?" Henry Harris asked.

"Not if you put your mind to it," Fred said.

"Could we learn?" asked Henry's brother.

The idea of teaching thrilled Fred. He would do for them what the Baltimore street boys had done for him.

"You can if you want to learn bad enough," Fred answered.

Good masters, like William Freeland, gave their slaves Sunday off to rest. Therefore, Fred decided that Sunday would be a good day for teaching. Of course, they'd have to gather someplace where their masters wouldn't find them. Here, as elsewhere, slaveholders wanted to keep their slaves ignorant.

Fred's school became very popular. News of it

spread from farm to farm. Before long he had forty pupils, and he succeeded in teaching most of them how to read. These results were remarkable because his students could not give full attention to learning. They were always afraid of being found out and punished.

Fred ran his school for the rest of the year. At the end of the year he returned to Thomas Auld's for the Christmas holiday. He felt happy about his school, but he still was enslaved, subject to his master's bidding.

The year 1836 started with Fred's condition unchanged. Mr. Freeland had asked for him again, and he was glad not to have to walk into a new situation. Once more he returned to familiar surroundings and to friends.

During the previous year, Fred had used the Bible as his teaching book, but now he used the *Columbian Orator*. As he went over the readings on human rights which it contained, they aroused him more and more. The Declaration of Independence, in particular, fired him to discuss escaping and freedom with his friends, Henry and John Harris.

"Thomas Jefferson said that all men have the right to 'life, liberty, and the pursuit of happiness,'" Fred explained. "We have life but not liberty. And we cannot seek happiness because we're not free."

"Jefferson said these things, but did he mean them?" asked Henry.

"Yes, he freed his own slaves," said Fred, "so he meant what he said."

Fred and the Harrises soon decided to act to secure freedom. They knew what they had to do. They would have to go "north," as far north as possible. They would have to get to a big city, where they might have a chance to get lost in the crowd.

It was actually only a short distance from eastern Maryland to the free states of Pennsylvania and New York, but Fred and his friends didn't know how close these states were because they had never seen a map. They were chiefly concerned about the dangers they would face along the way—hunger and thirst, traveling through strange country, and wild animals.

Anyone might face such hazards making a trip on foot. For escaping slaves, however, there were extra hazards. These included slave hunters armed with guns and dogs that might tear a victim apart.

Fred and the Harris boys were aware of these dangers but were willing to face them. They took as their rallying cry Patrick Henry's "Give me Liberty, or give me Death!" Another enslaved man, Sandy, who had given Fred the "magic" root, begged to be included. Fred, remembering Sandy's kindness to him, reluctantly agreed.

The group planned carefully. They would take a large canoe on the shore of Chesapeake Bay and paddle to the head of the bay. There they would land, set the canoe adrift, and start northward on foot, using the North Star as their guide.

The group chose the Saturday night before Easter Sunday as the time for their departure. Both Sunday and Monday would be holidays, so they would not be missed for at least two days. Fred also wrote out passes for the others, signing them with their masters' initials. These would protect them if somebody stopped them before they got far. The passes read: "This is to certify that I, the undersigned, have given the bearer full liberty to go to Baltimore for a few days to spend the Easter holidays."

Everything went well until the morning they were to leave. Then suddenly at breakfast time, a group of white men armed with chains and whips appeared. "We are betrayed!" whispered Fred. "Swallow your passes!"

Soon it became obvious that Sandy had betrayed them. He was the only person not captured and bound. The other three, including Fred, were dragged fifteen miles to Easton. There they were put in jail, each in a separate cell.

The usual penalty for this sort of crime was sale to traders in the deep south states of Georgia, Alabama, Mississippi, and Louisiana. Slave life there was reportedly worse than death, and escape to the north

"We are betrayed!" whispered Fred. "Swallow your passes!"

far more difficult. Thinking that this sort of life was in store for Fred and his friends made Fred feel miserable. He had gotten them into it.

Everything turned out much better than they feared, however. Since they had swallowed the passes, there was no proof they had planned to escape. Their masters, knowing that they were good workers, decided to keep them.

Fred's fate was in the hands of Thomas Auld, who considered his arrest the last straw. "I can't be bothered with you any longer," he said, "and I won't have any peace as long as you stay in the neighborhood."

He paused, giving Fred a little time to worry about what he might say next. Then he added, "I've decided I was a little hasty in taking you away from my brother, so I'm going to send you back to Baltimore. Now that you're nineteen years old, it's high time for you to learn a trade."

Chapter 13

North to Freedom and a New Life

Hugh Auld found Fred a job as apprentice in William Gardiner's shipyard in Baltimore. Supposedly Fred was to spend his time learning how to caulk ships to make them watertight. That was not what happened. When a rush order came in, Fred was told to help the carpenters. He was often asked to do several things for different men at once. The carpenters grew angry when Fred did not do what they asked, and eventually one and then another hit him. Fred hit back. The men then ganged up on him and beat him badly.

Mr. Auld could do nothing but not require Fred to return to Gardiner's shipyard. Instead he took him to a place on Fell's Point where he himself worked as a foreman. By now he had lost his own shipping business and had to work for others.

In his new situation, Fred rapidly became an

expert caulker. By the end of the year he was earning the highest possible wage for the trade in Baltimore, a dollar and a half a day. Even though he earned this money, he could not keep it. All the money he earned had to be turned over to his master. This was one of the cruel and unfair facts of slave life.

From the other caulkers, who were free men, Fred learned about the East Baltimore Mental Improvement Society where they debated the issues of the day. He met with the group often and made many new friends. Constant companionship with freemen and free women made Fred more and more dissatisfied with his lot. Why should he be a slave, and they be free? He felt that he was as good as they were.

He started to make careful plans to escape. As a first step, Fred decided to acquire some money of his own. He learned that other slaves hired themselves out, giving their masters a fixed sum at the end of each week. If a slave made more than enough money to pay his master, he kept the extra amount.

Fred tried to get permission from Hugh Auld to hire himself out. Finally he convinced Mr. Auld that the arrangement would be beneficial to both of them. He would board and clothe himself and give Mr. Auld the prescribed amount every Saturday night. Formerly, Mr. Auld had been responsible for all of Fred's keep.

Once he had some money saved, he still needed a safe way to go North. He asked his friends, and the freeman who finally came to Fred's rescue was a sailor whom he had met on the docks. This sailor, knowing that a traveling black man could be asked at any time for his "freedom papers," offered Fred his own seaman's papers. He himself could get others, he said, on the ground that he had lost the original ones.

On Monday, September 3, 1838, Fred said goodbye to Baltimore and to the life of slavery he had hated and resented for so long.

He reached New York safely, but suddenly his joy was diluted. By chance he met another fugitive slave, named Jake, whom he had known in Baltimore. "New York is full of Southerners who have come up here on trips," Jake said. "And there are many free black men here who act as spies. They hang out on the wharves and in the railroad stations, waiting to catch runaways like us. Don't trust anybody!"

For several days Fred wandered around like a lost soul, sleeping in doorways and eating only what he could buy from street vendors. At last he decided that in spite of Jake's warning he had to trust someone. Finally he explained his problem to a friendly sailor.

Again luck was with him. The sailor took him to David Ruggles, who helped to manage the underground railway, an undercover means of helping slaves escape to the North. He took Fred to his home and found him temporary work.

Fred poured out his life story to Mr. Ruggles. He even told him about Anna, a free woman he had met at the Mental Improvement Society, saying he hoped to marry her someday. He hoped that Anna could come up North, too.

"We'll get her up here so that you can marry her," said Mr. Ruggles. "Then we'll help the two of you go on to New Bedford, Massachusetts, where most people are abolitionists. Besides, New Bedford is a whaling town. You'll be able to find your kind of work there."

Soon Anna came up from Baltimore and she and Fred were married. Then they took a steamboat from New York to Newport, Rhode Island, where they transferred to a stagecoach to complete their trip to New Bedford.

When they arrived at New Bedford, they were met by another underground conductor, Nathan Johnson. A new last name was necessary, Johnson explained, because the name Fred Bailey would be too easy to trace.

"How does the name 'Douglass' sound to you?" Nathan Johnson asked. "Douglass is the name of a great character in a book that I'm reading, called *The Lady of the Lake*."

Fred felt that it would be a good omen to take

on a literary name, and Anna readily consented. Accordingly, from that moment onward Frederick Bailey, the slave, ceased to exist. In his place, Frederick Douglass, a free man, came into being.

In New Bedford, Fred worked hard but had little time or energy for anything else. Then a young man gave Douglass a copy of the *Liberator*, an abolitionist paper edited by William Lloyd Garrison. As Douglass read this paper, he was fired with an excitement such as he had never known before. The *Liberator* demanded nothing less than the complete emancipation of every enslaved person everywhere in the United States.

Douglass waited for announcements of all anti-slavery meetings held in New Bedford. He attended the meetings, listened to the great speeches, and applauded their words with enthusiasm. But for the first three years of his free life, he never spoke up for the cause.

In the summer of 1841, when he was twenty-four years of age, a grand anti-slavery convention was called on Nantucket Island, with William Lloyd Garrison as the chief speaker. Douglass had never taken a holiday since he arrived in Massachusetts, but he decided to attend the meeting to see his hero in person.

When Douglass arrived at Nantucket Island, a man from New Bedford, who knew his story, asked

At first his voice cracked as he spoke, but it soon smoothed
out as he warmed to telling the story of his life.

him to tell the audience about his experiences as a
slave. Douglass trembled at the thought of speaking
to a large crowd, but he allowed the man to lead him
to the stage.

At first his voice cracked as he spoke, but it soon
smoothed out as he warmed to telling the story of his
life. He soon realized that he had the sympathy of his
audience, for he heard shocked exclamations and even
sobs. When he sat down, he was dripping wet with

perspiration from his ordeal, but he was happier than he had ever been before.

At the close of the meeting, Douglass was asked to become an agent for the Massachusetts Anti-Slavery Society. His job would be simply to go about the state telling his life story. It was felt that no one could plead the case against slavery as eloquently as someone who had actually lived and suffered under it.

Douglass could not refuse, for his heart and mind were both dedicated to the ideal of freeing the slaves. He was careful, however, as he went about the state, to use fictitious names and places. He hoped that these would mask his identity should the Aulds hear about the fugitive slave who had become a public speaker.

In this way Douglass began the work for which he is still known today, as one of the most eloquent opponents of slavery.

What happened next? Turn the page to find out.

What Happened Next?

• In 1845, Douglass published his *Narrative of the Life of Frederick Douglass, an American Slave* and went to England to lecture against slavery. His book quickly became a bestseller.

• Fred founded and ran a newspaper, *The North Star*, in Rochester, New York. He continued to speak publicly against slavery and help escaped slaves traveling on the Underground Railroad to Canada.

• After the Civil War, Frederick Douglass campaigned for the 14th and 15th Amendments, served as an advisor to several presidents and as U.S. Consul-General to Haiti, and spoke out for women's right to vote.

• On February 20, 1895, Frederick Douglass spoke at a meeting held by the National Council of Women in Washington, D.C. That night, he died suddenly of heart failure.

For more information and further reading about Frederick Douglass, visit the **Young Patriots Series** website at www.patriapress.com

Fun Facts about Frederick Douglass

• Frederick Douglass, the man who was once sold to the highest bidder at a slave auction, eventually became the trusted advisor to presidents Ulysses S. Grant, Rutherford B. Hayes, and James A. Garfield.

• President Benjamin Harrison appointed him Consul-General to Haiti.

• When Frederick wrote his autobiography, he took great care to leave certain details of his escape out of the story. This, as he explained, was done so that the slave owners knew nothing of the particular steps he took to escape and could not keep other slaves from doing the same.

• In 1838, Frederick took the last name of Douglas, which he spelled "Douglass," from a character in Sir Walter Scott's poem, "The Lady of the Lake."

• A clay pitcher, on which is an image of Frederick Douglass's head created by an unknown artist during Frederick's lifetime, is displayed in the National Museum of American History in Washington, D.C.

• Frederick Douglass was the first African American to buy a house in an area in Washington, D.C., restricted only to whites. His 21-room home, called Cedar Hill, is now a National Historic Site and contains 1,200 books, all part of Douglass's personal library.

When Frederick Douglass Lived

Date	Event
1818	Frederick Bailey was born into slavery in Maryland.
	• James Monroe was president.
	• There were nineteen states in the Union.
1826	Frederick's new mistress Mrs. Auld began teaching him how to read.
	• Former presidents John Adams and Thomas Jefferson both died on July 4th.
1838	Frederick successfully escaped to freedom in New York and changed his name to "Douglass."
	• Samuel Morse demonstrated the telegraph in public for the first time.
	• John Wilkes Booth, Abraham Lincoln's assassin, was born.
1845	Frederick published *Narrative of the Life of Frederick Douglass, an American Slave*, the story of his life.
	• Macon B. Allen became the first African American lawyer.
	• Texas was admitted as the 28th state in the Union.

1848   Frederick Douglass attended the
            nation's first Women's Rights
            Convention.
            • Gold was discovered in California.
            • James K. Polk became the first
              president to be photographed in office.

1870   The 15th Amendment, for which
            Frederick campaigned, was ratified,
            and, from then on, African Americans
            were allowed to vote.
            • Virginia became the 8th state to be
              readmitted to the Union after the
              Civil War.
            • Mississippi elected the first African
              American U.S. senator.

1872   The Equal Rights Party nominated
            Douglass for vice president of the
            United States.
            • The first National Black Convention
              met in New Orleans.
            • Susan B. Anthony, famous women's
              rights leader, was fined for trying to vote.

1889   Frederick Douglass was appointed U.S.
            Consul-General to Haiti.
            • North and South Dakota, Montana,
              and Washington became states.

1895

- Thomas Edison showed the first motion picture.

Frederick Douglass died in Washington, D.C., February 20th.

- Grover Cleveland was president.
- There were forty-four states in the Union.

What Does That Mean?

abolitionist—person who believes in doing away with slavery

about-face—a complete change in attitude, behavior, or point of view

aft—toward the stern (back) of a ship

apprentice—young person bound by a legal agreement to work for another person in order to learn a trade

brandishing—waving angrily

callousness—lack of feeling

clairvoyant—person who claims to be aware of things others cannot see

cooper—person who makes or repairs barrels

fictitious—not real

impudent—rude

jib—small triangular sail on a sailing ship

larboard—left side of a ship

larder—room where food is stored in home; pantry

poultice—medicine on a cloth applied to the body to relieve pain

pupil—student

scow—a large flat-bottomed boat used for carrying freight

sloop—sailboat with one mast

starboard—right side of a ship

About the Author

Elisabeth P. Myers was born and reared in Grand Rapids, Michigan, graduating from Vassar College with an English/Creative Writing degree. She took several post-graduate courses at SUNY Buffalo and Northwestern universities. She married a professor of Accounting and Finance right after college and lived with him in Buffalo, New York, Wilmette, Illinois, and Bloomington, Indiana. She has one son, an anthropologist, and one grandson, a historian.

Myers has had 21 books published, all of which are biographies for young people. She has written verse for the *Buffalo Evening News*, travel articles for *The Chicago Tribune*, novel adaptations for high school textbooks, and a variety of short stories for a number of children's magazines.

Myers loves to travel and has visited all 50 of the United States, often "in the footsteps" of people about whom she has written. She has been to 92 countries and has taken cruises on the Amazon River, the Baltic Sea, the Caribbean Sea, the Mediterranean Sea, and the Mississippi and the Ohio rivers.

Myers says, "I enjoy writing for children because they are such an eager audience. It has always been a pleasure to visit schools and talk to students about what interests them. I have a collection of letters that some of them have written to me."

Books in the Young Patriots Series

Volume 1 *Amelia Earhart, Young Air Pioneer*
by Jane Moore Howe

Volume 2 *William Henry Harrison,
Young Tippecanoe* by Howard Peckham

Volume 3 *Lew Wallace, Boy Writer*
by Martha E. Schaaf

Volume 4 *Juliette Low, Girl Scout Founder*
by Helen Boyd Higgins

Volume 5 *James Whitcomb Riley, Young Poet*
by Minnie Belle Mitchell and Montrew Dunham

Volume 6 *Eddie Rickenbacker, Boy Pilot and Racer*
by Kathryn Cleven Sisson

Volume 7 *Mahalia Jackson, Gospel Singer
and Civil Rights Champion* by Montrew Dunham

Volume 8 *George Rogers Clark, Boy of the
Northwest Frontier* by Katharine E. Wilkie

Volume 9 *John Hancock, Independent Boy*
by Kathryn Cleven Sisson

Volume 10 *Phillis Wheatley, Young
Revolutionary Poet*
by Kathryn Kilby Borland and Helen Ross Speicher

Volume 11 *Abner Doubleday, Boy Baseball Pioneer*
by Montrew Dunham

Volume 12 *John Audubon, Young Naturalist*
by Miriam E. Mason

Volume 13 *Frederick Douglass, Young Defender
of Human Rights* by Elisabeth P. Myers

Watch for more **Young Patriots** Coming Soon
Visit www.patriapress.com for updates!